HEDGEHOGS

DIANA WEBB

Bill Buckets and the Magnificent Marrow

illustrated by
Alicia Garcia de Lynam

HODDER AND STOUGHTON
London   Sydney   Auckland   Toronto

British Library Cataloguing in Publication Data

Webb, Diana
    Bill Buckets and the magnificent marrow.
    I. Title   II. De Lynam, Alicia Garcia   III. Series
    823'.914 [J]
    ISBN 0-340-50167-7

Published by Hodder and Stoughton Children's Books,
a division of Hodder and Stoughton Ltd,
Mill Road, Dunton Green, Sevenoaks, Kent TN13 2YA

Photoset by En to En, Tunbridge Wells, Kent

Printed in Great Britain by Cambus Litho, East Kilbride

The mums and dads and teachers were doing special things to raise funds to pay for a new swimming-pool at Hilltop School. They were having jumble sales and fêtes and barbecues. Swimming-pools are very expensive.

'More work for me,' moaned the school caretaker, Bill Buckets. But he didn't really mind. He was delighted that the children were having a swimming-pool.

Then the headmaster thought of a new way to raise money.

'Each class will grow a marrow in time for Harvest Festival,' he announced. 'It will be a sponsored marrow grow. The children can ask their families to pay the school a few pence for every kilogram their marrows have grown before we pick them.'

It seemed a great idea. So eight classes planted eight marrows in the school garden.

'We'll pick them on the first day of the autumn term,' the teachers told them.

'Who will water them in the holidays?' said the children.

'More work for me,' moaned Bill Buckets. 'But don't worry. I'll keep an eye on them.'

The children collected the names of all their relations who wanted to support the marrow grow. And they wrote down how much each person would pay. Some had very long lists. Others weren't so lucky.

10

'But it all adds up,' said Bill Buckets.
And meanwhile the marrows were
growing.

Bill Buckets' wife Matilda thought it was funny. 'The marrows are trying to get fat. But I'm trying to get thin. I'm on a diet,' she laughed.

This gave one of the children, Ben, a new idea. 'We could ask our families to promise a few pence for every kilogram Matilda loses,' he said.

And some of the children did just that.

'If I promise the school any more money, I'll have to rob a bank,' said little Lindy Brown's granny.

Soon after that the holidays started.

The children were curious about their marrows. When Jimmy Smith and his friend Ben went past the school on their bikes and saw Bill Buckets in the playground, they said, 'How are the marrows, Bill Buckets?'

Bill Buckets went a little pink. 'Don't ask questions,' he said.

Jimmy and Ben were worried about the marrows now. They went round to the back of the school and climbed up on the wall to look in the garden.

'One, two, three, four, five, six, seven,' they counted. Seven of the marrows were still there. But the marrow their class had planted had gone. Class eight's marrow had completely vanished.

'Someone's pinched it,' they gasped.
'But who?'
    'It can't have been burglars,' said Ben.
'Prince would chase them away.' Prince was
Bill Buckets' dog.
    'So was it his sheep or his goat or his
pig?' said Jimmy.

'No,' said Bill Buckets sadly as he came
up behind them. 'I'll tell you who it was.
It was Matilda's mum who picked it.
She didn't know it was special. But she knew
Matilda was slimming, and she knew
marrows don't make you fat. So she picked
it as a treat for Matilda's lunch. She's ever
so sorry.'

Jimmy and Ben helped Bill Buckets plant another marrow for class eight.

'But how will it grow fat and heavy in time, like the others?' they wondered. 'Our class will blame Bill Buckets if it's no good. And we don't want Bill Buckets in trouble.'

Jimmy and Ben were dismayed.

But meanwhile Bill Buckets was up to something very mysterious in his friend Bert's greenhouse.

'Don't you ask me about that marrow,' he said to Jimmy and Ben when they went past on their bikes again.

On the first day back at school the headmaster said in assembly:
'Now is the time to weigh the marrows.'
Jimmy and Ben held their breath.
And into the hall came seven children carrying seven large marrows.

'But there's a bit of a problem with class eight's marrow,' said the headmaster. Jimmy and Ben felt sick.

Then into the hall came their marrow. It was enormous. It was gigantic. It needed three people to carry it. A little boy, Bill Buckets and Matilda were staggering under its weight.

'Gosh, my granny *will* have to rob a bank!' gasped little Lindy Brown.

'Three cheers for Bill Buckets!' cried Jimmy and Ben. 'He's the one who kept an eye on it.'

'Three cheers for my special super-strength fertiliser,' whispered Bill Buckets.

At Harvest Festival seven marrows were
sent as presents to old age pensioners.
But Bill Buckets took class eight's marrow to
the county show, where it won first prize.
It was on the nine o'clock news, too.

'It could be the heaviest marrow ever,'
said the newsman. 'And all because of a
special super-strength fertiliser.'

'*Secret* super-strength fertiliser,' said Bill Buckets. 'Only I know the ingredients and I'm not telling anyone.'

Thanks to the giant marrow, the children collected pounds and pounds. There was nearly enough money now to pay for the swimming-pool.

'I just managed to stop my granny robbing a bank,' said little Lindy Brown.

The children were still bringing in money for the swimming-pool during the winter. The building went on well in the spring. And at the beginning of the summer term there was a grand opening ceremony with a bathing-beauty contest.

'Who's that strange lady in the leopard-skin bikini?' asked the judge.

'That's not a strange lady,' said Bill Buckets. 'That's Matilda. She's been eating that marrow all winter. She's lost loads of weight.'

BEAUTY CONTEST

Matilda won first prize in her leopard-skin bikini, but it was not real leopard skin. And the children who were collecting money for every kilogram that Matilda lost went round with a tin and filled it with money.

'Hurrah! At last we've reached our total. The pool's paid for,' announced the headmaster.

'It's a good job you kept an eye on that marrow, Bill Buckets,' said the children.

'It's a good job I kept an eye on Matilda,' said Bill Buckets.